P9-CSF-710

SUPER

JAPAN

1150X2.1TX22.2H

VOG

VOG

OFF BAKE BROIL CLEAN
COOK TIMED
SELECTOR

The Perfect Purple Feather

BY **Hanoch Piven**

English text by Rachel Tzvia Back

Silhouettes by Janet Stein • Photography by Adi Gilad

Megan Tingley Books

Little, Brown and Company

BOSTON   NEW YORK   LONDON

Copyright © 2002 by Hanoch Piven
English text by Rachel Tzvia Back

First published in Israel in 2000 by Am Oved Publishers Ltd. Tel Aviv

First English Language Edition

Library of Congress Cataloging-in-Publication Data

Piven, Hanoch.
    The perfect purple feather / by Hanoch Piven ; [English text by Rachel Back].—1st
English language ed.
        p. cm.
    Originally published: Tel Aviv : Am Oved, 2000.
    Summary: Rhyming text and illustrations take the reader on a journey, in which a
simple purple feather becomes a whisker for a cat, a pen for an owl, a quill for a
porcupine, and more.
    ISBN 0-316-76657-7
    [1. Feathers—Fiction. 2. Animals—Fiction. 3. Stories in rhyme.] I. Back,
Rachel Tzvia. II. Title.
    PZ8.3.P55868417 Pe 2002
    [E]—dc21   2001038401

10 9 8 7 6 5 4 3 2 1

FC-China

Printed in China

The illustrations for this book are photographs of three-dimensional collages created from
found objects and glued on watercolor paper painted with gouache.

The text was set in Frutiger Regular, and the display type is Alor Bold and Remedy Double.

"Please give me that feather you hold in your hand,
So I can fly in a flash to a faraway land."

"Scat! Fly away," meowed a black catty cat,

"That feather's for me—anyone can see that!

It brightens my whiskers, a look quite unique—

With that purple feather, I'll be very chic!"

A porcupine said glumly, "It's a sad, sad life.

No one will hug me—I'm as sharp as a knife.

But with that feather, I'd be soft and so sweet—

I could charm anyone I happened to meet."

Declared the centipede, "IT'S JUST NOT FAIR.

I have lots of legs, but not one little hair.

If I had that feather, I'd primp and I'd preen.

Why, I think I'd feel just like a queen!"

An ant crawled to the centipede's side,
"HEY, COME WITH ME, WE'LL GO FOR A RIDE.
That feather will help us sail far away—
Come, climb aboard—it's a beautiful day!"

A loud owl scolded, "I'm old and I'm wise.

THAT FEATHER'S FOR ME—IT'S NO SURPRISE.

I'm a great writer, and here's what I think:

That feather will make a fine pen for my ink."

"Hey, Jacob," chirped a bluebird in a nearby tree,

"I'M MISSING A WING—JUST LOOK AT ME!

The doggy next door feared being left out,

So she yapped at the owl and said with a pout,

"Give me the feather, which waves like a flag.

I'll make it my tail and give it a wag."

SUDDENLY, THE BEDROOM SHOOK WITH A ROAR—

As a black and gold tiger pranced through the door.

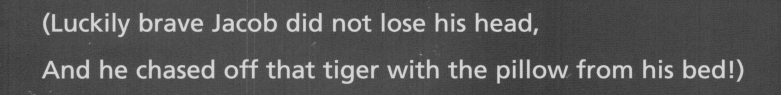

„That feather will make a fine toothpick to munch—

After I've eaten that doggy for lunch!"

(Luckily brave Jacob did not lose his head,

And he chased off that tiger with the pillow from his bed!)

Just then a mischievous tick butted in.

He picked up the feather and said with a grin,

"What a great feather—it's as soft as a rose—

I'll use it to tickle that elephant's nose!"

The elephant giggled and rolled around on the floor.

Over and over she rolled toward the door.

CHOOOOO

Then she raised her trunk high and—**AH, AH, AH**

OOOOOOOOOOOOO !

SHE SNEEZED THE MOST MAGNIFICENT SNEEZE!

It was so amazingly loud, it shook the tick's knees!

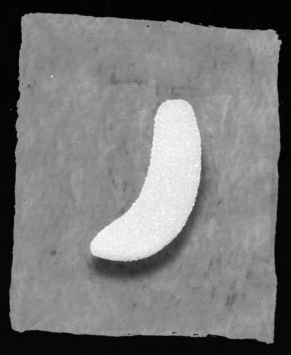

He sat wide awake in his dark little room
And saw out his window a bright yellow moon.

A perfect purple feather!

"How cool!" said Jacob. "So silky and sleek.
I like how this feather tickles my cheek!"

Jacob tossed and turned in the middle of the night—

Something seemed different, not quite right.

He felt a prickle at the back of his head—

Something was poking from the pillow on his bed.

HE PULLED IT AND PUSHED IT AND PULLED IT SOME MORE.

What he had in his hand, he couldn't ignore:

Out flew the feather and it wafted up high.

It twirled and it swirled through the dark-blue night sky.

Jacob thought about the feather,

Then he pondered some more.

Soon his eyes gently closed,

And he started to snore.

And the perfect purple feather? Where did it fly?

Past the yellow moon? Higher up in the sky?

Perhaps it will end up somewhere nameless and new.

OR MAYBE IT WILL LAND . . .

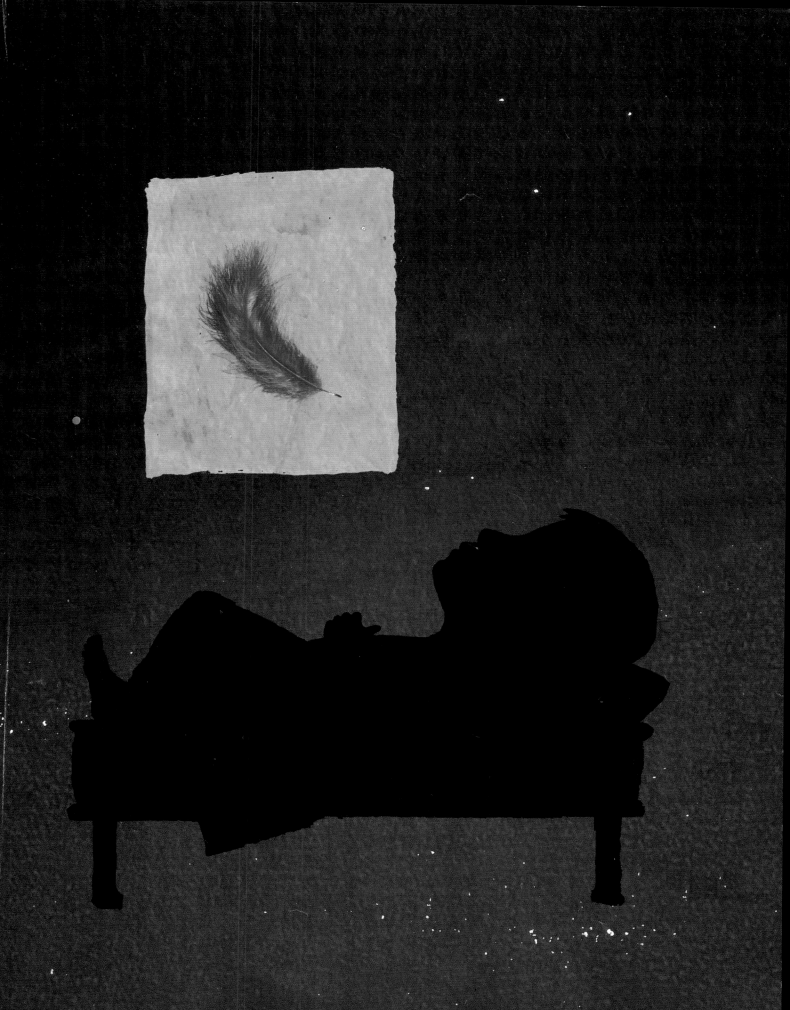

right here with you.

To my three purple feathers

—H. P.